Ian Whybrow

Tim Warnes

Say Boo
to the
Animals!

Sandy Creek
NEW YORK

Ready, steady, off we go!
Creep through the woods on tippy-toe.

We're off to meet some animals, and when we do
If you see a scary one, just say **BOO!**

There's an owl, up a tree.
I wonder if he's after me?

To-whit!
To-whoo!

We're not scared of you, **BOO!**

Help, a monster's on the loose!
Quick! Say boo to the mighty moose.

Stamp!

Stamp!

Stamp!

We're not scared of you, **BOO**!

We're not scared of you, **BOO!**

What's that creeping down the road?

Let's say boo to the warty toad!

Croak!
Croak!
Croak!

We're not scared of you, **BOO!**

Here's a thumper and a thriller!

Now say boo to the giant gorilla!

Thump!

This is where the tiger lies.
Let's give him a big surprise!

We're not scared of you, **BOO!**

Baby wolf cub wants to play.
He's not scary – he can stay!

Just in case you're not quite sure
Let's hear your loudest **BOO** once more.

For my *vicini cari* the Viazzani children, Valentina, Adelaide,
Emilia and Giacomo – who will all please read this in turn to
Clementina until she is *annoiata fino alle lacrime* or *blu nella faccia*.

I.W.

For Jacob, with love from Uncle Tim!

T.W.

Sandy Creek
NEW YORK

An Imprint of Sterling Publishing
1166 Avenue of the Americas
New York, NY 10036

Text copyright © Ian Whybrow 2008
Illustrations copyright © Tim Warnes 2008

ISBN 978-1-4351-6509-0

Manufactured in China
Lot #:
1 3 5 7 9 8 6 4 2
01/17

www.sterlingpublishing.com